CW00520098

A BIRMINGHAM STORY

RYAN SINCLAIR

ISBN:9781973492207

DEDICATION

This book is dedicated to everybody who's ever felt overwhelmed by emotions whether positively or negatively and has struggled to deal with them. For all the triers, doers, believers and achievers.

CONTENTS

SHARING WHAT'S SPECIAL

WORDS IN VISION

This book studies the unique emotion based friendship between three childhood friends who have gone in separate paths throughout their lives. Despite being in different positions and making different choices, they come to an understanding they've all faced similar challenges; yet have all dealt with them differently. This book was inspired by an analysis of my own life specifically from a teenager to a 24-year- old, and how society labels those who display emotions and/or types of behaviour.

Kyle aims to get back in touch with one of his two best friends growing up. Having grown up and become happier with himself since he's been away. He begins to make plans to move back. Awaiting a reply, Kyle remains optimistic.

OPTIMISM

Some would Say I represent optimism at its finest,
Because whether rain or shine,
My ambition stays vivid in each and every climate.
I'm not sure if there is a ladder to success,
But I'm willing to find it and then climb it.
Or something of that sort,
I can taste success I'm just preparing for it with my napkin and my fork.
I know there's always a reaction to each and every thought.
So my plan of action is to stand by my statements, like a solicitor in court.
And that's just how it goes,
I think I get it from my environment,
Mom always told me she had no regrets upon her retirement,
You were the first person I called when she passed; there was a lot of screaming and dialing,
But time is a healer, and soon became my requirement.
But that was 4 years ago and now I'm 26,
Being open-minded breeds so many benefits,
Been through too much already with my little brother, and his mental wellbeing is delicate.
A contrast from mine, I truly believe that I can win the lotto,
My advantage is my mind, Strong like rum out of the bottle.
Wray and nephews perhaps,
Sometimes in life, the best defence is attack.
And by that, I mean to protect your spirit and attack your goals,
I use to drink spirits and it attacked my soul.
It affected me, matter of fact,
I neglected me.
And that's why I'm here, to let you know,
There's more to life than just digits and stacking notes.
I just hope this text receives you well and you pick up the phone,
And tell everybody I've been thinking a lot about Birmingham and moving home.

Slightly overwhelmed by a shock text message, Carl decides to respond to Kyle after some time.

SURPRISE

Sorry for the late reply,
I've been preoccupied,
And 4 years have gone so quick,
I know it's near the anniversary of when your mother died.
I miss her too, but never mind that,
It's the age of instant messaging what took you so long to type back?
DELETE DELETE DELETE Maybe I shouldn't type that.
It's good to hear from you too I know it's been a while,
And Michael is okay he's just seen his child.
Enter this earth, must be a strain on the purse strings,
Can you imagine a little Michael earthling?
With his eyes and nose and cursing?!
Though inside I think something is a little concerning
He's struggling to pay his bills now he's no longer earning.
His anxiety is unreal,
When your happiness is your child,
But the prices at McDonald's don't seem like a happy fun meal,
You slowly realise happiness isn't money, but no funds isn't how fun feels.
Anxiety and Depression kills and slumps; more people nationally than any gun will.
And I think he's suffering through this,
He finds it hard to connect with reality and there's no buffering through this,
The last loan I gave him was like a student loan to students.
Long gone within an instance,
It is like his mind is long gone within the system,
Single father,
Maria left him, now she's long gone within the distance...
I think she contributed to the plight of him,
Not being able to provide for your child is enough fear to frighten men,
I just feel with you back around,
He might be alright again.
It's crazy how life is always asking you some kind of question,
Cash didn't build our bonds and I ain't talking about investments.
You need to come back as soon as you can,
So we can help out our brethren.

Having heard a reply from Carl, Kyle is surprised and thus wants to gather more information.

He decides to reach out to Michael and attempt to show some love,

and let him know he is there for him during this tough period.

LOVING

Michael, it's Kyle what's going on?
I know it's been a while but I've heard what's been going on,
Bits and bobs but second -hand information is always wrong.
So I thought I'd come directly to you,
And understand for myself,
And I understand if you think I'm just for myself,
But Carl says you're struggling and you needed some help.
Generational wealth was our mission,
But I'm concerned about your mental health and if it goes missing,
Then I need to intervene. Love you like a brother,
But I cannot be a spectator to these scenes,
And act like things are the same as when we were teens.
Time goes on, but it is what we do with it is the key.
I'll be moving back to Birmingham in the next 1-2 weeks,
And I think it's really important that we do meet,
You may argue I haven't been in your shoes,
But we wear the same shoes on our two feet.
Our history runs too deep.
I've heard you're a father too, I knew you'd come round to the idea,
Now in a few years, our kids will be on the playground while were in Ikea.
My son was 1 last week and I can still recall when I cried tears,
Of joy, my first boy, helped suppress some of my fears.
Because I dedicated my whole life just for making his better,
And stayed away from distractions,
His life is priceless to me so gambling mine was like playing with fractions.
Understand the love means more than the fabric so I invested my few pennies and paved a way into fashion.
It started out John, Mo, Carl, Me, You
Just some teens with dreams of being adults now were closer to three-two,
Now Mo and John are gone, but anyways I'll explain more when I see you.

Michael receives this message but is not impressed or in the right frame of mind
to converse with his soon to be returning old friend.
With his own life crumbling around him, he isn't bothered about anybody else's.

DEPRESSION

So after all this time you get back to me,
In the time since we last spoke I could have met the pope and built my own factory.
I've heard money isn't happiness, but why don't you send some my way and look after me,
Because financially and mentally I'm locked up in her majesty's faculty.
Or at least that's how I feel anyway,
I'm a single pringle father now ever since Maria went away,
I'm stressed out and ready to pop like a can of lemonade,
59p a can, feels like the weight of a beer can and it's not like I'm getting paid.
Unemployed father, can't even buy his daughter toys father,
Doesn't have the cash to go out and drink with the boy's father.
Disappointed like when I realised as a boy I had a void father.
But besides this, I'm doing the best for my kid,
Though she cannot speak yet, I can see what she's trying to say in between her eyelids.
'Mommy's going to be back soon' is the excuse that I give.
I'm not only lying to myself, I'm lying to her,
And I'm not only crying to myself, I'm crying with her,
And this amongst other reasons is why I prefer silence to words.
But despite that, I'm glad you're returning back to the city,
A bit of positivity goes a long way,
Remember when we used to chill by Snow Hill?
Matter of fact it's been a long day.
My phone line might cut off in the next 24 hours,
So if it does come to my house; same address as always.

Depressive thoughts just become the norm for Michael
as he slowly gets accustomed to negativity.

SADNESS

Thanks for turning up I thought it was Kyle at the door,
I feel like I've had enough, excuse the mess I've been lying on the floor.
I feel like he wants to know if I'm coping socially,
But my emotions are like onions,
The more I peel the more tears fall inappropriately.
He tried to motivate me like a life coach,
But I don't think there's any coaching me.
Sometimes In life, things aren't what they're supposed to be.
Now I see you want to interrupt me, but you'll get your chance to speak,
See inside something erupted me, and even when I plan to sleep,
My mind is dysfunction-ing and even can retreat,
Me and my daughter are more similar than I thought.
She can't walk and I can't get on my feet.
I just don't know where to turn anymore,
Nothing besides her is my concern anymore,
Life problems rain on me and then they pour.
But yes please continue, and speak from your chest,
I need to feel what's within you, I trust your word more than the rest,
I'm sorry if I seem blunt, I'm just full of stress.

Realising what he has said to Kyle might upset Michael,

Carl decides to visit Michael to see if he can speak some sense into him.

Frustrated by Michael's negative outlook, Carl lets him understand this and how they actually share more similarities than Michael would have imagined.

TRUST&FRUSRATION

What you're saying is true, but I don't know how to say it to you,
Frustrated I can't help you more, most nights I end up praying for you.
Trust the energy that you send out to the world you will receive back,
Don't get mad I'm just giving you some feedback.
You're my best friend since school, but I am not willing to argue with you about these facts.
And that's partially why I get frustrated,
Because I'm a dreamer with no receipts for my risks and just payslips,
And each day I put on a fake smile like I had a facelift.
I'm just as unhappy as you but my problems are lesser than yours,
I make excuses and compare my life to others, I guess they're my flaws.
I know I hide it well...
Even though I can feel the stress in my pores.
And that was hard to share,
This life is priceless and I can't watch you waste it like a Cartier,
We've each got our own issues,
And at some point, we have to face them although that may be hard to hear.
And the way you described your conversation with Kyle it's like you hardly care.
Your daughter is your seed, and you harvest your own landscape so put a farm in there.
Maybe I'm the wrong person to give you the right information,
But that's why I brought him into the equation.
If you really think I'm gonna sit here and watch you sink further into negativity,
You better phone a friend who's not 50/50 and come and get rid of me,
We don't need to be millionaires to reach victory,
You just need some guidance and support and the rest is history.
And I know it seems like a lot of stress,
KNOCK KNOCK
Oops, I think that you've got a guest,
We'll continue this convo just hold on a sec.

Kyle is local and full of happiness and ready to catch up with his old friend Michael.

He hopes to galvanize and motivate him to do something about his predicament.

Though Michael is full of envy.

HAPPINESS&JEALOUSY

Kyle-Hey, before you say it: yes I know I've finally arrived,
I know times have changed but there's nothing like spending time with the guys.
Is Michael inside? Because I've brought him a beer,
It was such a long drive Carl, I would have got you one too if I had known you were here.
I know you're not a heavy drinker, and I don't either,
But breaking the ice can be like breaking an ISA...
Account.
Plus the amount only came to a fiver.

Michael-So you've finally arrived, it's like the return of Guy Fawkes,
I know you're living life but you'll need to come off that high horse.
If only my reality was compatible with your kindness and nice thoughts.
But this is the reality I was explaining to you,
You've been back 2 minutes and I'm already complaining to you,
For you to understand about my life,
You'd have to dig a ditch and then have some abseiling to do.

Kyle-Bro, you need to change your prerogative,
Like you said you have a daughter and you've got a lot to give.
The reason I returned was to help you out this predicament.
But it seems as though the struggle is something you'd rather be sticking with.
And that's just me assessing the energy you're giving off,
4 Years of being out the city,
But the time I've spent with you has been a lot.
And you were never this negative,
Even when you got arrested at 16 and had to stay with relatives.
So tell me everything you need to share because I wanna know everything.

Michael-First of all, I didn't ask you to come back,
I might be struggling but I would never have done that.
You really think you're better than me,
Why? Because you've got a successful business, family and your relationship isn't in the cemetery.
Well, things change, and talking like that will put our friendship in jeopardy.
You must think I'm some centipede, crawling through life who tends to grieve,
When things don't go right.
In fact, I think you should leave and assess your own life.
You act like you can't be wrong, and you only know right.

Fearing his two close friends' discussion is going to escalate, Carl steps in.

FEAR

Guys chill, what kind of reunion is this?
Bickering like what we used to do as kids.
Nobody's better than anybody and nobody wants to struggle,
So giving a hand is not a hand-out if you come from the same rubble.

Michael, already upset by Kyle's earlier comments;

he lets him know exactly how he feels in no uncertain terms.

ANGER

With all due respect Carl, me and Kyle have drifted apart,
Growing up, most people couldn't tell the difference apart.
Now he wants to come into my home and criticise my energy,
Lost all respect for you Kyle so I don't care for what you're telling me.
You think your word is science,
But you're the one who in school failed chemistry.
I'm sick of your systematic strategy to build status,
Even when I was 16 you were the one to give statements!
Three nights I was in that police cell, I hope that you sleep well,
Because you owe me some favours!
You talk about us wearing the same size shoe,
Well from when I was a youth my clothes were tailored!

Kyle listens to what's said and offers a courageous response.

COURAGE

So now we've got to the root of the problem, the problem is me?
Well, being a potential inmate on a joint enterprise charge was not what I wanted to be!
I had greater ambitions & goals,
But YOU would rather listen to those,
Who'd take you down the wrong road and that became a problem for me.
You can't disguise your jealousy through having a problem with me.
I'm happy to help but you need to take control of your emotions;
One moment you're happy I'm returning next moment you're provoking...
I know we've become distant, but I find it insulting;
That you'd be willing to cut off somebody that wants to see you growing...

Finally, having heard enough, Carl drops a bombshell of his own.

I'm honestly concerned with the breakdown in communications,
This isn't what I came for,
You guys are both fathers complaining about how you treat one another,
But neither of you lost a child at age 4.
Why do you think I'm full of pain for?!
I say less and try and stay busy to forget, while you guys do less and say more.
You both don't even understand how blessed you have become to see your children grow in your vicinity,
I hardly even know mine,
And honestly, the thought of that is killing me,
All because of MY ego, I had no balls like Luis Figo,
I couldn't be bothered to stay connected to her mother like a line of symmetry.
So, tell me what do you have to complain about?!

Realising, he shares similar experiences as Carl.
Michael can't hide his anxiety for what his friend is going through.

ANXIETY

So, you're a father too? Now it all makes sense,
Even though currently I struggle to pay rent,
I'd rather have my daughter's nappies than the smell of regret as my fragrance.
And when you said you were just as unhappy as me,
Inside I started sarcastically laughing you see,
As I couldn't imagine somebody being in a worse situation than mine,
That thought process became a habit to me.
But despite all that.
I've got my ray of sunshine that reminds me of what I'm fighting for,
That's my motivation I can't fathom the frustration that you might endure.
I mean, everything we discussed was just as relevant to you,
But you decided to hold it in,
Just thinking of not meeting my daughter gives me the chills all the way from my feet to below the chin.
Your exterior is still young, but your soul is growing old within,
You need to work out your differences with your baby's mother and pull up like when you go to the gym.
All this time you were looking out for me, you were speaking to us both,
Your heart was yearning, and the blood was seeping down your throat,
As every word you said was like a knife slicing through some toast.
Enough about me, how do you really cope?

Carl demonstrates how he copes day to day with his problems.

GRATITUDE

By wearing this face, and being full of gratitude,
By focusing on what I have instead of what I don't have is what I have to do.
Thank you for your input, I feel like the roles have reversed,
Maria left you, but I'm the real one left in the dirt.
I do need to work out my differences, I guess we're one and the same,
But with most of this being my doing, how can I complain?
Swallowing my pride is something I just have to decide to do,
Instead of trying to tell you what's right for you,
I need to make amends and get to know my daughter,
And become a less spiteful dude.
Because I know I'm in the wrong.

Trying to add a positive spin to their situations,
Kyle aims to raise the spirit as the three prepare to embark on a new beginning.

POSITIVITY

With all the aggressiveness and negativity in the room,
I just want to say a few words you both can consume.
I know we've each had our differences and challenges,
But despite that, we're all still here and slightly managing.
Even though listening to both of what you said were damaging.
We all went different directions,
But it's the same struggles we've been dissecting,
Struggles, loneliness, depression?
The universe brought us back together as we've each tried progressing.
Childhood friends, adulthood companions,
Standing in the same position like mannequins.
But now it's time we elevate individually and collectively,
As I want the best for you both and I'm sure you both want the best for me.
So, let's achieve what we set out to before we rest in peace.
And show the world what Brum boys are really made of.

Shortly after their reunion, Michael, Carl and Kyle each head back

to their own personal lives in a new mental space after a very emotional reconciliation.

Though things are not perfect in each of their lives,

they all reach the understanding that a problem shared is a problem halved.

And that ultimately, they are just energy beings.

THANK YOU

Firstly, and foremost, my mother Thelma. My initial and consistent inspiration for furthering my poetry. You saw it from the beginning, as a youth using writing to express my feelings and troubles up until this moment. Unconditional love.

My big brother Daniel. More like a father to me growing up and constantly looking out for me and supporting me with how I can take this project further forward.

The Birmingham Poetry Jam Scene, thank you for giving me the confidence to share my poetry to you in large audiences on a month by month basis.
Anxiety still challenges me when performing live but without you and the experiences I've had within your environment I may have never allowed my voice to be heard.

ABOUT THE AUTHOR

Ryan Sinclair is a poet, a TV background artist and a youth mentor from Birmingham. He has been writing poetry from his early teens after using it as an avenue to express his feelings and emotions after his brother was nearly murdered. After a few years hiatus, Ryan regained his passion for writing whilst studying at university and wanted to put his regained energy for words into a vision. He has featured in local newspapers when a teenager for his poetry.

CONTACT

Wordsinvision.co.uk
www.Facebook.com/WordsInVision
www.Instagram.com/Wordsinvisionart
www.Wordsinvisionart@gmail.com

Printed in Great Britain
by Amazon

62591883R00024